THE STORY I TELL MYSELF ABOUT MYSELF

SARAH LAYDEN

Sonder Press

Sonder Press
New York
www.thesonderpress.com

ISBN 978-0-9997501-2-4

First U.S. edition 2018
Printed in the USA
Distribution via Ingram

Acknowledgments

Thank you to the editors of the following journals, where these stories first appeared: *Booth, PANK, Wigleaf, Anderbo.com, Pindeldyboz, Midwestern Gothic, failbetter, kill author, Vestal Review, Fiction Southeast, Metazen, Punchnel's,* and *Contrary.* "The Woman Who Was a House" and "The Woman with No Skin" were also reprinted in *Not Like the Rest of Us,* the bicentennial anthology of Indiana writers, published by INwords Publications and the Indiana Writers Center.

Thank you to Elena Stiehler and Sonder Press for bringing this manuscript to life. Thanks to Barbara Shoup for the continued support and writerly inspiration. I'm also grateful to Steve Fox, director of the Hoosier Writing Project, a site of the National Writing Project. Some of these pieces were born in HWP, an immensely valuable writing and teaching workshop.

Love and thanks to my dear family: Tom, Trevor and Brendan.

For my parents

THE STORY I TELL MYSELF ABOUT MYSELF

CONTENTS

HANG UP

FOR FIFTEEN YEARS HE'D carried her phone number, checking every so often to see if it had changed. In this way he followed her from Binghamton to Boston to Chicago, and then to a suburb outside the Loop once she'd married and had children. He'd call from payphones on business trips, listening to the outgoing message on her machine (cutesy, including the cat's name, Whiskers. He'd thought her more original than that. But no: Whiskers.)

They had failed together. They had been together and failed. Together they had been failures.

At first, they had not. How else could it be? They had punctuated one another's lives at a distance, over the phone they had made each other weep with near-identical histories of loss, they had winked into the mouthpiece, imagining they could be seen. They were seen. She made up for him a series of stories about an elephant who could speak, a bandit who stole ladies' undergarments, a couple searching the world for a person who had allegedly died but might still be alive. She had been recovering from a storm of death swirling around her, young death, and the stories helped. I'll take care of you, he said. With a finger, she traced and retraced his words on the inside of one wrist, which she stared at with longing when he failed his promise. He still called, a silent reassurance. He still called, picturing her all the time, naked, when he was alone, which was all the time.

Back then, grief had made her easily weak. Someone who

flopped into arms as if in a faint, who landed in beds because they were soft. The dark hid her expression. He'd ask, Are you crying? And she'd lie, I'm happy. Make no mistake. When a woman cries in bed, she misses the missing. Now when he called and hung up, he hoped she cried in bed and thought of him. But she no longer cried in bed.

Of course it was him. No one else would want to know her yet be so incapable of succeeding. In the few seconds' pause between "Hello" and the hang-up, she conversed with dead air. A few words at first, then whole sentences, then stories. One about a girl who cut off her hair to give to birds. Another about a stranger on a bus who carried a newspaper umbrella, which was covered in headlines of sorrow. And that old story, her favorite, the couple's mission to disprove death. She told her husband and small children that she was a volunteer storyteller for shut-ins. A little true.

Home alone, she gave the female characters her name and the male characters his. She paused, waiting for the click. Sometimes it came in the middle of a story, sometimes not at all. They waited one another out. Each one alone, thinking: Don't hang up. You are the story I tell myself, about myself. Stay with me. Stay.

DE|COY

THE DUCKS WALKED ON water atop a scrim of ice, wings unfurled like biblical robes. Orange feet no doubt turning blue. From Alice's house, they appeared to hover: the indecision of flight.

The babysitter was late. She had texted fifteen minutes ago to say as much, fingers on the keypad in her car. Seventeen years old and she would claim to have been at a stoplight, obeying the no-texting law. Right. Alice had been seventeen once. Granted, seventeen without a cell phone. They existed, she just didn't happen to have one back then. Still, she remembers the mostly-harmless lies she spun like cotton candy, camouflaging her whereabouts and companions and choice of outfit. Now there were phones everywhere, phones with cameras. The lies should have been more elaborate but somehow grew blander. *Had 2 get milk 4 my mom! Sorrreee…*

Alice's screen remained black, no follow-up from Brittany, a cease-and-desist from the small thoughts sent from phone to phone, brain to brain. She thought, we are in one another's heads. We are giving each other access to the workings of our minds. Tapping out codes in butchered English. Like perfectly good furniture that's intentionally been made shabby. There was a store in the mall that sold high-end furniture, weathered on purpose. Dressers appearing to have been beaten with pine boughs and scuffed by expert hands wearing sandpaper gloves, then sold for way more than they were worth. David's new apartment was furnished with a few such pieces, spare save for his sleigh bed, his rough-hewn farm table and benches. Alice had glanced around quickly when dropping Sylvie off for weekend visitation with her dad. She managed to see enough.

Outside the breakfast nook window, the pond ice glowed in the dusk like Ice Capades, a trick of the orange and purple sunset. Alice had a date tonight. The ducks were indifferent, hopping and splashing, trying to warm up, or maybe not. They were cold-blooded. Sylvie had fogged the window with her breath that day, laughing for the first time in a long time, watching the ducks shake the water off their backs. She arranged her rubber duckies on the windowsill, hoping to attract the real thing. No dice. The males—drakes, Alice remembered, not from school but from watching Sesame Street with her daughter—crowded the lone female. Alice bunched the cotton placemat in one hand, checking the time. Sylvie was bathed and pajamed and already in bed. Nighty-nighted and lullabied. Asleep both times Alice checked on her. These rare nights out only happened after Sylvie was asleep.

The babysitter was half an hour late. Maybe Brittany had a new boyfriend. Once the babysitter got a social life, forget it. Alice had been that kind of teenager. And she often suspected the motives of the majority of the world's population. Not without cause. People wanted to pull one over on you, hide from you their true hearts. They only wanted to give you so much, though sometimes you wanted—needed—more.

Or they gave you too much, as a month of online dating had proved. Information you didn't care about or need to know. What they were or weren't wearing. How they were or were not damaged by the people they had once trusted. Details that were almost always revealed too soon. She shut down her online account after the free trial ended. Tonight she'd have dinner with Bryce, five years out of the state university's top dental hygiene program, who had cleaned her teeth the week before. You could get Botox at the dentist, not that she wanted it. Not, Bryce said, that she needed it. That vertical line on her forehead was easily hidden beneath bangs. (So much for growing them out.) The face ought to map your life, she thought. It ought to look used. What happens if you erase what you've been? She was not ready to forget.

David had moved out three months ago. He would've left sooner but it took time to find a place close to what was now Alice's house. Close to work, too. Which meant close a particular woman he worked with. Alice had had a hunch, a sense something had been amiss. David didn't admit anything, but he agreed it would be good for him to leave. So he left. Sylvie missed her father. She sometimes cried out for him in her sleep. She sleepwalked, and on several occasions Alice had woken to find her small daughter curled like a puppy in front of their bedroom door. Her bedroom door. At daycare, where Sylvie once painted and sang and drew pictures and cooked in the play kitchen, she now clung to her mother's pantyhosed leg and sobbed.

Alice stood and walked to the front window, circling the hall like a cat. Damn Brittany, and damn Bryce, too. Truth: She no longer wanted to see either of them tonight. Brittany smelled like Diet Dr. Pepper and baby powder and irresponsibility. Bryce's hands spent their days in other people's mouths. Those hands had been in her mouth. Would he charge a late-notice cancellation fee, as his office did? Alice reached for her cell phone and headed outside to the driveway for better reception. The stars were coming out, pinpricks of dazzling light so distant as to be unreal.

She was still staring skyward when the pond ice cracked, loud as a snapping tree branch. Early thaw, those ducks, the flap and honk as they sent themselves skyward. The front door gaped open; she had closed it, or maybe not. And in that moment, the one that arrives before knowing, she imagined Sylvie with the yellow quilt pulled to her chin, her breathing deep and rhythmic, her mouth open. When the babysitter pulled into the drive, headlights panning over the pond out back, Alice, racing to her daughter's bedroom, was not there to see.

THE REST OF YOUR LIFE

IN AN HOUR, YOU'RE scheduled to learn about the rest of your life.

It's all mapped out: a twenty-minute drive north through the winter sleet. A left turn at the looming hospital building. Before entering, you refresh your lipstick in the parking lot. This is going to be the kind of day you might look back on, thinking, at least I should've worn some lipstick.

The elevator crawls to the fifth floor. You are glad to be alone in this mobile box. Out of habit, you tilt your head back and wink at your reflection in the mirrored ceiling. Partly for luck, partly in case the mirrors are two-way. Somebody must work elevator security, staring at small grainy screens, at the tops of joyless people's heads. All dandruff and baldness and crooked parts.

At the fourth floor the car halts. The door swooshes open, and a kohl-eyed woman wrapped in a multitude of multicolored scarves jingles inside. Her stooped, aged body is made of silks and linens and elaborate wraps. You feel overdressed and stuffy in your black wool coat and gray scarf. She is from inside, you are from outside. The elevator resumes its upward trajectory until the woman extends a bangled wrist and pushes the STOP button.

"You come here to find out something," she says in a thick, hard-to-place accent. "Why is it you want to know?" She is petite. Her long dark hair has surprisingly little gray. Her skin folds and twists, making shadows across her face when she gives a quick, upward wink at the mirrored ceiling. For this, you trust her. You take a deep breath, just like the doctor who examines your chart. (Or body. Same difference.)

"I want to know whether I'm..." you begin.

"No," she interrupts. "Not what. Why?"

The accent could be Romanian. She could be a stage actress. A paid participant in an elaborate prank, in cahoots with a cameraman hidden behind a two-way ceiling mirror. There are fingerprints on the edges of the glass.

"Can you tell me? Do I get to ask three questions? Or make wishes?"

"Already you ask three questions," she chastises. "And please to come off of it. This is not like the Disney movies."

She fiddles with the elevator buttons. You are descending. "Better we should go," she whispers. "That I can tell you."

The two of you march stride for stride across the lobby linoleum. A man calls out, "Mariska!" But she does not turn. She threads her arm through yours, a thin silver bangle pressing into your wrist's skin. She tightens her grip and twirls you around and around, a maniacal square dance. Beneath her knitted shawl you glimpse the pale green hospital gown. Then the world—the glass doors in front of you, the bank of elevators behind—blurs. No longer do you know what you face.

"Here is the rest of your life," she says, spinning you. "The rest of your life is here."

WHAT | MARY DID

KNEELING IN THE FRONT row is Mary, a woman with the reddest hair you've ever seen. Supernova hair. Light eyebrows, an ethereal movement to her hand when she touches her forehead, chest, left shoulder, right shoulder, almost as if she's forgotten they are parts of her body. The touch reminds her.

She stands in boots not meant for church, a full three inches taller than the priest who doles out the communion she does not take. The parishioners say the priest resembles Gregory Peck; Mary is too young to know who that is. It is Wednesday, and for the third day this week Mary has left work and come to Mass, suddenly appearing among the devout retirees like a baby in a basket. They can't help but touch her hair when it is time for the sign of peace. They whisper in her ear, *Peace be with you.* They glance at their fingers as if expecting to see red.

She has not showered in three days. She will not return to her home; a man still lives there, but who is he? She sleeps in her car. Sponge bathes in the office restroom, daubing her body with wet paper towels that leave cold gray spit wads under her arms.

At communion she does not take the host. Ida Mae Tucker, supplicant, creases her forehead in Mary's direction but won't make eye contact. Mary bows slightly, leaning her head to the priest. Gregory Peck blushes to the tips of his ears, thumbs the sign of the cross on Mary's bluish-white skin, the translucency of low-fat milk.

THE STORY I TELL MYSELF ABOUT MYSELF

Someone has spray-painted over the inspiro-religio query on the concrete overpass Mary drives beneath on her way to Mass: What Will Gordon Do? A man by that name lives in the house she left. He told her to go, she left, these are just words. The dark moon beneath her index fingernail looks like black spray paint, or earth.

Mary, a shade dyslexic but never diagnosed, thought as a child that Jesus was spelled Gees-us, like the Bee Gees. In school she was shaky with tenses. Still. She does not care what Jesus or Gees-us or Gordon or any of them *would* do. (She already knows. He confessed; it has been done. An admission allowing him to take communion.) Mary wants to know what will come next. Facts hard as concrete. Permanent as painting on a bridge, until a new tagger comes along.

No one in this church has heard her voice, raspy with cigarettes, unintentionally seductive just like the rest of her, save for those boots. They did not see Mary leaving her home days earlier, her hips simply moving the way they move—I can't *help* it, she would sometimes tell the man who still lives there. They see her eyes on the ground. They consider her holy, submissive. It's just those boots, Mrs. Tucker complains to whoever will listen, and nobody does.

SEX IN SECRET

BACK THEN WE COULD have sex in secret. We weren't projected onto screens, held captivatingly in shades of blue and white. There was no blog text pix wall comment update reply-all. There was only a room with a door, and sometimes that room was a car. We could still grab the cold metal handle, pull it towards our chests. Steam up the windows. We were inventive back then, not like today. Now you can thumb a ride on the information superhighway. Wear revealing pixelated trousers, displaying skin that a few years back would've burst into flames with the slightest UV exposure. We wanted to see that skin, yes we did. We saw that skin. But it wasn't through viewfinders and lenses and night-vision goggles. We saw that skin with our own eyes, felt it with our own hands, the softness radiating, wearing down our fingers with repeated touch, back then, in secret.

We climbed together into beds made for one person, we kept our shirts on but not our pants, our pants on but not our shirts. We took showers separately and dangled thick strands of wet coconut hair into the faces of whoever was lying below, a mouth in a dimly-lit room grabbing the ends and pulling, pulling, bringing our faces closer, into a kiss that tasted clean and dirty at once. Wet hair slid easily through lips, each strand in place. Candles burned on the nightstand, a fire hazard, reason to be on the lookout. We would doze and wake and begin again.

The door was shut. Closed firmly, even locked. No one would

have entered. There was only us. One of us, both, checked the latch to be sure.

After, we called, or we didn't. We didn't call.

Before, there had been only the room and the people it contained. The door slammed upon exit, even if you could picture the inside, the blood-red comforter and Chianti bottle used as a candleholder, even if you remembered the small mouth and ripped T-shirt and black sweatpants, but couldn't envision the face. Even if the room reassembled itself electronically, and in those pixels you saw your name and what you did with whom, back when we made use of ourselves silently.

Now, we post instantaneous mobile uploads of the Chianti bottle to prove its existence before proof is called into question. We reconstruct the past into permanent electronic skyscrapers, erecting landmarks which scroll what has come and gone. We wave tattered flags made of undergarments. We create hyperlinks leading to one another's genitals. We use rudimentary Googling skills to find and find again, clicking easily.

We still don't call. There are no secrets left for us to share.

HE WAITS, WANTS

HE SHOWS HER THE calendar: it's Day Fourteen, so they must have sex. Doctor's orders. His cycle changes each month, but this morning, when he held the stick between his legs and peed, the window showed two lines for imminent ovulation.

In the mirror, he stares sideways at his abdomen for signs. He gropes his flat, hard pecs searching for tenderness. His hopes rise and fall with the moon. She murmurs, Next time.

He's already told her what color to paint the guest room. Best he's not around the fumes. The paint, a designer concoction specially mixed at the superstore, is a sunny yellow. He corrects her: Gladiola. Hands her the paint chips and an instructive list. Gladiola, he repeats.

Some nights, she'd rather keep her clothes on and watch *Lost*. Or slip out to the corner bar. In the dusk, the birds will twitter at her, sounding surprisingly like the music in her head. She tries not to skip down the street. Turn the corner, the bar suggests, and you disappear. Your house can't see you.

It's Day Fourteen. The pharmaceutical company in Waltham, Massachusetts, manufacturer of a variety of sticks you pee on, trumps biological instinct. She could tape *Lost*. She could go to the bar afterwards. But post-coitus, he must remain flat on his back for fifteen minutes; won't she stay? For once? In the past she'd jump up to use the bathroom, make a snack, open a beer. She hates how he raises his pale legs in the air, as if her juices need gravitational guidance to marinate his hidden, impenetrable barren places. Legs like white flags, surrendering dignity.

He complains, lying prostrate, "I just saw the future. I'm tied down and you can roam." She doesn't correct him, only says, "Back in a minute." She returns carrying two drinks, and an inward sigh of relief. He is right, that isn't her future. She spills a little gin on the good sheets, toasting: "At least you can still drink." He eyes the droplets. "At least it's clear," she says.

The programmatic sex regimen makes her forgetful. Check the calendar. Light years from their first summer together, when they made love wherever and whenever she, both, wanted. Now he takes his temperature each morning. He alludes to mucus in places she doesn't want to think about him having mucus.

The Meyer kid got knocked up at sixteen. Jealousy swallowed her each time she saw him mowing the lawn shirtless, his pregnant belly taut and tanned, hanging over his cargo shorts. Even if she'll never have that, she wants to take her top off outside. To expose her paleness to the sun. To walk bare-chested in a summer downpour, rivulets of water running between her breasts.

Meanwhile, he monitors himself. He waits, wants. He can't know: she used to still does always will want a baby more than he does. This is her secret, like cells multiplying inside her, what she carries instead of their child.

COMET'S RETURN

THE NIGHT OF THE funeral, after emptying the house of mourners and clearing away the trays of deviled eggs and ham, Davey heads outside to wait for the comet's return. He sits in the empty truck, makes it less empty.

Just this morning, the hearse had dwarfed its occupants, the driver in the black cap, the cargo in back. Davey had driven his mother, they were second in line in the funeral procession, and could see the parted, yellowed hearse curtains and the wooden casket carrying Davey's father, Hy, whom despite it all Davey idolized: Davey who is nearing forty and still scandalizing women in town. He turns his Ford's ignition key and thinks about the coffin, oblong, and the hole dug by the gravediggers, and how the coffin—and his father—fit in that hole as if they had been born to do so (and they had.)

He'd changed from his polished black shoes and suit into his standard uniform of jeans and work boots, a heavy sweatshirt. He carried a thermos of coffee and a flask of whiskey. A blanket. A brown paper sack with some of the leftovers made into a sandwich. His many aunts and uncles, morose over the passing of their brother, had perked up considerably when the deli meats and rolls were placed on the table by his mother's well-meaning friends. Except Aunt Delores, who at fifty-four was still referred to as "the baby."

"Your father loved ham salad," Aunt Delores sniffled, chewing slowly. She idolized her brother Hy. She'd been fifteen when Davey was born. Still liked to buy him outfits, shirts and pants which usually matched.

The truck, parked beneath the old linden tree his father planted twenty years ago, turns over once before starting. Davey lets the motor run a few minutes and cranks the heat against the April chill. It is now three-thirty in the morning, and the comet is scheduled to show by four. Last time it came around, Davey was five years old; his dad had been twenty-two, strong enough to carry him to the barn turret where he instructed Davey to watch carefully. Davey glued his eyes skyward. "What did I miss?" he kept asking. It became a family catchphrase. Hy, sauntering in after being gone a few nights, would ask the same thing.

The coffee in the thermos rolls easily down Davey's throat, strong but not good. He scans the sky for nothing.

Earlier, his Aunt Mary leaned over the couch and confided, "You're turning out just like Hy." Stared at him levelly, cool, cocking one eyebrow. She did not elaborate. They'd just buried a man who had charmed everyone from his own family to the postman while secretly drinking himself to death. Who claimed to have been faithful to Davey's mother. But on the form, the coroner checked "multiple causes," indicating otherwise. Davey did not know people still got the disease his father had got. In this day and age, he heard his mother say, not shocked. Days before the funeral, the health department distributed leaflets in the Stop-N-Shop.

His loyal closemouthed aunts, they'd known. Hy's drinking had led him to other places, inside himself and elsewhere. Where do you find whores in Podunk East Jesus, Uncle Robert asked, his pet name for this small, upstate farm town. He seemed genuinely curious, as if whores were on his shopping list for the day's errands. A voice came from one of the helpful women in the kitchen, half-joking and half-sanctimonious: There are whores among us.

Davey stares into the black sky, seeing not the stars but the day in pieces, his life in pieces. At the viewing Tina Shea sidled over and put her arm around his waist, nice and low, his mother oblivious and his aunts frowning, and he could not think of his father's graygreen face in front of him. He had mentally acknowledged that he was not thinking of his father but of Tina, the way she felt beneath his hands, the lack of limits to her willingness. And here she was now, in his head as he stared blankly at the blank sky, trying to conjure his father.

Peripherally, he catches the movement of some nocturnal creature. Davey cranes his head out the side window, searching for a coyote skulking in the brush. In the corner of his eye comes a flash like a weak camera, a trick, and he retrains his gaze on the night. What did I miss, Davey mutters aloud, out of habit. A phrase he originated and his father copied, a question with more answers than either could've fathomed

THE WOMAN WITH NO SKIN

FAR AWAY OR UP close, she appeared just like anyone else: a young woman with pale arms and legs, a milk-face unblemished by a single freckle or pimple or blotch. Only when she turned a certain way did it become clear that what rested atop her muscle and bone was not skin, but a kind of permeable membrane through which anything could pass. She could not sit outside in spring, for the pollen would swirl in the air and attach itself to her very insides, moving in such a way that suggested her body was no barrier, that it was barely there at all.

Clothing helped, but sometimes the fibers lodged deep. And she did not want to cover herself completely. She wanted air. She wanted to let the world in. But the problem with the world was that it wanted to be let in all the way.

Her friend was a scientist and designed for her an eco-friendly brown polymer suit. He had the garment specially fitted, yet it sagged at the waist, suggesting the figure of a doughy gingerbread woman. She wore it to the mall. Teenagers with vulture-like scapula asked, "What's with the jumpsuit? Do you, like, drive a racecar?" For once their comments didn't travel directly through cardiac muscle, or wend their way around chutes of gray matter. The words stuck to the suit. The young woman felt cautious elation. She spent free evenings wandering the city in blank bliss. Within weeks, the polymer carried so much text it looked like a newspaper.

THE STORY I TELL MYSELF ABOUT MYSELF

Curiously, she wanted to read her body. She returned to the mall to stand before the three-way mirrors. She couldn't discern the crowded words stuck to the left shoulder, so she unzipped the suit, just a little, at the neck. Suddenly the flood of voices inched inside.

I adore you. Don't make this any harder. Please come in immediately to discuss your blood work. I think we both know this isn't working. Cruelty-Free Chickens, $4.99/lb.! *We regret to inform you that your brother...*

She didn't know who was speaking, she didn't know when the words had latched on. She grabbed the zipper, which stuck, so she yanked downward to loosen the teeth. Soon the brown polymer gaped open and she could see the membrane, the un-skin, pummeled by the accumulated gusher of words. An ocean in her ears, like listening to a conch shell attached to headphones with the volume on high. So loud she could hear nothing.

In the mirror she met her own eyes. The suit hung loosely around her waist, the zipper finally freed. Her body a bruise. She held the metal pull-tab lightly between two fingers. She silently asked her reflection a question, then watched and waited to see what she would do.

THE WOMAN WHO WAS A HOUSE

THERE WAS A WOMAN who was a house.

Not as big as. Was. A vinyl-sided exterior coating her limbs, a sloped roof over her head. Her insides made of wood paneling, framed, dusty pictures hanging on the wall of her chest cavity. Clinging to the back of her pelvis, a collection of Civil War-era spoons, family heirlooms.

A projector shone its light from her lungs, powered by her breath. The projector played home movies, vacation slides. Kodachrome past lives. A version of herself that she scarcely remembered: a clapboarded teenager ambling stiffly along the beach on a family vacation. Back in her cottage days. Now she stayed put, having grown into something closer to a Victorian.   Her attic-brain stored forgotten things nobody wanted anymore. Wardrobes filled with her parents' mothballed clothes, decades of polyester and lamé; they'd taken the Civil War uniforms. Her little brother Abe's tricycle, unused for decades. Boxes upon boxes, black-markered "Memories" in her mother's scrawl, filled with photo albums, scrapbooks and postcards. The old newspaper clippings with their sensational headlines.

All the lives lived in this house. Her family, sheltered for free and saving on mortgage payments, now come and gone, migrating to the Caribbean without her. "You can't exactly move a house," they said. "Here. Have these spoons."

THE STORY I TELL MYSELF ABOUT MYSELF

She'd seen houses moved before: power lines lowered as a loaded flatbed trailer inched down the pike. She imagined the warm-belly feeling of a family still inside, a fire in the fireplace and smoke snaking up the chimney, though of course that would be unsafe. The family would be driving behind the flatbed in a station wagon. The fire would have been extinguished the night before. Her own family had burned many fires in her fireplace, esophageal soot that still rose up, now bitter.

Probably you could move a house on a boat, down to a Caribbean island.

Maybe. "But how would we pay for that?" the family asked. "Be reasonable."

"We could sell the spoons," the woman suggested.

"Those spoons have been in the family for years! You should display them in your house with pride!"

And so she did. They clinked when she shifted and settled, reminding her that she was not particularly interested in Civil War history. Her family planned the first underwater reenactments; Abe had gotten SCUBA certified. The island had no re-enactors, no connection to the Civil War, up until now. Which made the gifting of the spoons all the more poignant.

Home alone, she breathed and ran the projector. Her parents smiling beside the heavy artillery cannon, Mama in her petticoats and Papa in his blue uniform and cap. Abe as a baby, the tickle of him scooting across her wooden floorboards. She saw herself, growing taller each year, adding square footage alongside the flaming red maple. For years her house-proud parents had stepped outside to film her. Now she could only imagine the projector light pouring from her windows, which nobody filmed, nobody saw.

THE NEW THING

THE PACKAGE ON THE doorstep glistened with newness, cardboard exterior overwrap notwithstanding. She had seen the truck coming, heard its low rumble. Doorbell rung, vehicle left running in the street, driver trotting lightly back to his high-perched seat, tipping one hand in a lazy wave when she emerged onto the porch. The new thing was here. It was not shopworn, or holey, or covered in dust, or creaky with disuse. It was not odd-smelling. She had been waiting all morning, tracking the package online from the distribution center in Louisville, to the receiving hub in Indianapolis, and finally to her local driver in Naperville. New thing. New new thing. Her new thing.

When she opened it, presto change-o would occur. A makeover without makeup, a sparkle sans harsh detergents. She would cast off the old like a second skin, slithering out of one suit and into another. A cleaner, more sharply-pressed suit. The new thing was not a suit.

She picked up the package from the porch. A sunny day; already the cardboard felt warm. Probably from the truck, as she had left the new thing sitting for only a few minutes. Her watchless wrist could not confirm this, but she knew. The new thing was not a watch.

The deliciousness of waiting. The incomparable quiet before the ripping open. The cardboard exterior overwrap like a loofah to the fingertips, rough enough to scrub off prints. She thought of bath salts, lotions, methods of exfoliation involving Japanese sea kelp that needed to be refrigerated before use. The new thing was not perishable. She could not taste it.

It was not edible, breakable, washable or returnable. The new thing was what it was. It was not a book of pithy, cloaked aphorisms that hid more than they revealed. It was not an almanac or a guide to living. It was not one-size-fits-all.

The new thing could stay new as long as she wanted. Power, she thought, comes from places other than electrical outlets. The new thing was not an electrical source, nor did it have a cord or a plug, three-pronged or otherwise. She could not listen to the new thing.

She brought the new thing into the house, to the never-used guest bedroom decorated in a "Springtime Meadow" theme. Her gift-wrapping station hung from the closet rod in a neat vinyl case. She placed the new thing on the tightly fitted wildflower-print bedspread and removed from the vinyl case a roll of brown craft paper, her sharpened scissors, and packing tape. The craft paper, bought new, gave gifts the look of recycling without actual recycling.

The new thing waited, still in its cardboard. Placing the package on the craft wrap, she wound the roll around until the paper was gone. She never needed the scissors. She taped the new package closed. With a black marker, she carefully printed her name and address on the package, then set off for the post office.

FUL FILLED

SHE WAS THE TYPE of _____ who didn't get enough _____ as a child, leading to unparalleled _____.

He spent _____ on _____, eventually exchanging it for _____. That _____ helped.

In her purse were gift cards worth _____. There was _____ she wanted to buy.

Ask anybody: _____ can be cured. Just _____.

Note the brigade of _____. They are not responsible for your _____.

If her parents had only _____ more. If his parents had only _____ less. If their parents had only _____.

Therapy can take the form of _____, _____ or _____. You pick.

At the _____ they bought outfits for walking around the _____.

THE STORY I TELL MYSELF ABOUT MYSELF

Preteens are surprisingly _____. Thirty-somethings are never _____.

The young grandmother loads her _____ with _____.

The cell phone hears _____.

This generation is about _____, _____ and high-grade weaponry.

It is _____ your fault.

Maybe you will get what you _____.

ARRESTED DEVELOPMENT

THEY SAID VERA WOULD grow. She didn't.

There was the time she got carded at Forever 21, where she was buying a new top. The clerk said it was to verify her credit card. He asked that she remove her thumb from the date of birth. She knew they were snickering behind her back. To be old, way older than twenty-one, and be so small. Like a child but with laugh lines.

A mosquito followed her into the shower, bit her three times while she was masturbating. Neck, upper arm, calf. The bite of God, telling her to stop masturbating. The tiptoed reach to adjust the shower head. Why the shower didn't wash the mosquito away, she did not know. Unfathomable, to stand beneath clean municipal water and feel that dirty.

There was no money, which surprised roughly no one since there was no job. There was television for inspiration, a standard cable package that allegedly saved dollars in the long run but mostly tethered her to a chair for hours at a stretch. Ho-Hos and Twinkies, a bottle of orange Fanta drunk with a straw. The waste of plastic straws. Too late now, she sometimes thought in the produce aisle of the grocery store, stocking the cart instead with boxes of cellophane-wrapped snacks from the lower shelves, the child's eye view. Bright cardboard packaging, empty wrappers, a trash can full of straws.

Vera was waiting for the knock at the door that would change her life, but usually it was the mailman with a package she had specifically ordered. Or Aileen from next door, wanting something predictable and neighborly, like an egg or a cup of sugar. Trying to hide her pity eyes. Trying to not look around the cluttered house through the open door. Aileen was always baking things and usually brought some over when she was done. Which was fine. But not life changing.

"Listen," Aileen had said one time, towering over her in the doorway. "I know a very good doctor. Can I give you his number?"

"Is he single?" Vera asked.

Aileen faltered. "Um, no. I believe he is married. I meant for...you know..."

Vera waited. Aileen chose not to finish her sentence.

"All the good ones are taken," Vera said. It was a line often repeated on the TV shows she liked to watch, where gorgeous average-to-tall sized women complained about their general lot in life vis-à-vis coupling with the opposite sex. Or the same sex, depending on the show.

She'd been small as a child, but nothing her parents worried about. All children were small, they'd rationalized to Vera when she asked why they hadn't done anything. Called a specialist, or at least helped her find a name for what she was. There could have been an operation, she found out later, but now she was too old, too grown. "Where would we have gotten the money for surgery?" her father asked, pushing open the screen door with a hand that held a Plen-T-Pack of beef jerky. Under the other arm he clutched two cases of Coors.

In her childhood, as a consolation, her mother had bought her horseback riding lessons, which really were pony rides. The horses at the stable were far too big. Vera had to stand on a small step stool, then the instructor gave her a leg up. Once her feet were in the adjusted stirrups, she rode in slow, plodding circles. Vera glanced over at her mother only once, saw the pity eyes, then turned her attention back to the ring. The pony's name was Clover. They circled for fifty minutes of the allotted hour, and though Vera tried to count the laps, she always lost track after fifteen or twenty. More often than not, she stopped before the time was up.

MARV'S | 11 STEPS

1. MARV, THROUGH THE DOORWAY, over the aluminum strip of flooring that divides the kitchen from the living room (designed to prevent tripping on uneven layers, but upon which Marv regularly trips), heading to the kitchen, the fridge, for another beer—toe to aluminum, he recrosses the threshold again without a bride, unless you count one of the cans as a sort of partner. Marv doesn't count the cans.

2. Where else was he supposed to go? Marv had shown up on Sheila's stoop despite her warnings, he'd walked right up to the red door and rang the bell. Sheila said he was "darkening her doorstep," even though there was no sun, no shadow, no light from anywhere but inside the apartment at 3 a.m., just the light she'd turned on for herself. She told Marv to leave and he'd stood still, not taking a single step away, even when Sheila hissed that she'd smelled him coming, and always would.

3. Listen—there are places and there are places. Marv went to the newsstand like it was church. He sidestepped the litter and the pigeon-detritus and hedged along the shelves, then back again. He read every newspaper headline, scanned each magazine cover, read the articles he thought were worth reading, which weren't many. Daily he paced this sidewalk, a short Marv-sized path worn into the cement; at least that's how the newsstand owner, Burt, must have seen it. Burt didn't seem to

mind Marv—the guy could maybe buy something a little more often, not just *Newsweek* but maybe one of the fancy-ass rags, the ones that cost Burt a fortune to carry, but hey, everybody needs a routine, and this guy, Marv, appeared to have a couple.

4.   The Renegade Bar's jukebox played that same song every night. "Gimme three steps, gimme three steps, Mister, gimme three steps toward the door." The bartender put the machine on shuffle and out came the song, like magic. Didn't matter if it was Sonja or Pete behind the bar pouring drinks, the song played. Or maybe it just seemed that way? No. Every night. And every time the chorus asked for that three-step head-start, with each cheerful pleading of the lead singer and his backups, Marv would resettle himself on the stool, clasp whatever type of glass happened to be in his hand, and answer them, "Nah, I'm staying right here. I think I'll stay right here."

5.   At the hospital, Marv had run so fast down the corridor that he'd left a rubber tread from his sneaker. When Marv finally got to the room, Sheila was curled up on one side. Marv was still laughing, giddy. "Where's the baby?" he had asked. And all Sheila said was, "Gone." He railed, "Why didn't you call me? Why didn't you call?" She pleaded, "I did, I already told you on the phone, Marv...It was a girl." His sneakers squeaked as he ran out, leaving another mark for somebody else to clean up.

6.   Unless he was working, Marv would rise from the chair in his apartment to walk the couple steps to the bathroom, but that was it. The rest of these days he spent in the ratty recliner, wearing a terrycloth robe, a stack of magazines on his lap. *The New Yorker, Atlantic, Time, Esquire.* He read every word. He slept. He read some more, returning to the same articles. Some of it he'd remember. He shuffled across the room in slippers, sometimes plucking Kleenex from the box. "If Sheila were

here…" Marv thought, longing and hate and love all confused together like something thrown up from his own stomach.

7.   There are only so many ways to say you're sorry—Marv knows that chocolates are cliché, so he goes for enormous mall-cookies with vaguely contrite messages he orders up in frosting. "I am a first-class dick." "Somebody should have stopped me." The teenage girl behind the cookie-counter giggles nervously, painting blue words. Marv promises this is "just between us." He asks the girl if she's old enough to get into bars. When she ignores him, he just hums to himself and rocks back and forth on his heels. The frosting smudges when she places the finished dessert in wax paper. "Sorry," she says, a word Marv understands even if he really doesn't know how to say such a thing. "Don't worry about it," Marv insists.

8.   Late, late at night—so late it is almost light, almost not night—Marv steps to the faint glow of the window and thinks about making coffee, thinks about getting help, thinks about the sleep that eludes him on nights like this. He then thinks about Sheila and all her self-help books, the counseling, the admission into programs where he was forced to admit his weakness. "Weakness," his father used to tell him over the rims of his glasses, "is the worst sin there is." "Stop your crying," he'd said. "Stop it now. That's better. How'd you like for someone to see you? You might well go ahead and die. But die strong, boy. If you do nothing else for me in this life, do that." Marv still wondered over his father's command, words following him like an echo, like a bottle-cap rolling down the street, like an industrial scent on a factory-town wind.

9.   "Happy Fucking Anniversary"—then, "Happy Goddamn Shit-Eating Motherfucking Anniversary!": these are the cards he would buy if anybody made them. There is no reason for that kind of cruelty; besides, it has been many years since they'd celebrated anything together, and it is

43

not even the anniversary of their now long-dissolved marriage. It is the anniversary of that day in the hospital, the day Sheila should have had the baby and didn't. He finds a card that wishes "A Very Special Eight-Year-Old" a Happy Birthday, spelled out in colorful balloons. Marv scrawls his name on it and licks the envelope shut. He walks down to the corner and drops the card in the mailbox. Days later the envelope returns through the slot of his own door with the red-inked stamp of a pointed "Return" finger. He'd forgotten postage; the envelope flap still smells faintly of whiskey.

10.   Marv's first dates are barely distinguishable from second and third dates. He meets women at the Renegade, until eventually they learn they should be anywhere else. "We never go places," complained one girl on their third date—Emily, barely twenty-one, who had shown promise by accompanying him home on the first date and every one since. "Oh yeah?" Marv challenged. He grabbed Emily by the upper arm, marched her outside the bar onto the sidewalk, then wheeled her around back into the bar, to the same cracked leather stools they'd been keeping warm on and off for the past couple weeks. Her biceps shone red through the next two rounds of drinks. "Don't ever say I don't take you anywhere," Marv said to her.

11.   Years before, as a joke, somebody'd affixed dance-step patterns along the Renegade's empty dance floor. The rumba, the cha-cha. Now Marv leads Emily out onto the floor. The jukebox is playing a song he doesn't know; it has a beat slow enough that he can shuffle Emily around, breathe in the scent of her herbal shampoo. He sighs Sheila's name into Emily's hair. She doesn't correct him, nor does she answer to it. Do they share more than they know? But even if they each want to be other people, with other people, and somewhere else, here and now there is music, music and someone, their feet stepping in the same cracked pattern.

COLLISION PHYSICS FOR THE MATH-AVERSE

TIMING SCENARIO 1: THE HIT absorbed by the small car with excellent safety features prevented the big car from hitting a third, uninvolved car: an aged hatchback that would've crumpled like a wadded sheet of paper. In that car would've been small children, a young mother cavalier with seatbelts. Her cigarette inches from the child in the passenger seat. The collision that would've pushed the glowing cherry directly into the child's eye. The collision that could've happened a mile up the road but was prevented by the driver of the small car leaving five minutes late (**Timing Scenario 2**). There was coffee to be drunk, email to be checked, breakfast nearly forgotten but a piece of bread quickly toasted, quickly eaten. An email reconsidered, edited carefully, then reworded. The momentary regret of hitting "send." The clock checked, the panic of where-are-some-socks.

Mass: Bigger cars have more mass. In a collision with a Crown Vic, the Crown Vic wins. Always. A massive car, it owns the road, even—especially— when it runs a stop sign, pushing the mass of the smaller car into the mass of a pine tree. First rolling over a big clunky object, the mass of the front bumper. When the wrecker arrived, the pine boughs sprinkled needles, amassing small piles on the wet winter ground. The car dislodged easily as a tooth.

THE STORY I TELL MYSELF ABOUT MYSELF

Gravity: Items traveled about the car cabin before landing about the floorboards. The scattered contents of an open purse (wallet, receipts, the doctor form), a CD (Peter Tosh, "Legalize It"), a cell phone. At the moment of impact, the driver saw only the backs of her own eyelids. Meanwhile, inside the cabin, the possessions hovered, a perfect equation of flight.

Pitch & Frequency: No scream. Just a single word shouted repeatedly, then hoarsely. No! No! No! No! No! The airbag's pop and hiss, smoke rising, the scent of gunpowder. A wheezy-whistle breath. No! No! No! No! No! See how much a person wants to live. Hear the fuss a person makes over death. Like death is a very, very bad dog.

Parallel Universe: The driver of the smaller car remained in bed, skipping the doctor visit entirely, opting instead for the latest issue of *People*, a pot of coffee, a couple cigarettes smoked next to the cracked bedroom window. Bored, the driver eventually climbed into the small car for a trip to the drugstore where she purchased dark chocolate, *US Weekly*, an embarrassingly large box of Super Plus tampons. Returned home, watched *Seinfeld* and *Golden Girls* reruns. Slept easily, not dreaming of the sound of crushed metal.

Escape Velocity: A bent frame maligns the driver's side. A shove, a crank, and the door slivers open. Had the car ever stopped moving, had the driver? But there she is, doubled over on a stranger's lawn, beneath a stranger's pines, free.

TWO HEARTS

THE BABOON NEEDED MY heart. The surgery was scheduled for Tuesday.

One more week of housing my own ticker, a healthy time bomb concealed beneath layers of muscle and skin and so much hair that my girlfriend called it a pelt. At home, shirtless, I would beat my chest with two fists to make her laugh. The self-defibrillator of virility.

I had known Sunny, the baboon, for a decade. I taught him American Sign Language, how to express his wants and needs. He'd been named Sunny for his upbeat disposition and can-do spirit. He took quickly to the thumbs-up gesture and used it throughout the day. He scolded lesser primates for throwing feces. He brought over a broom and dustpan, whispering into their velvety ears, applauding when they sought it out themselves.

His favorite sign was "more," two hands tapping together at the fingertips. Vegetarian lasagna? More. How about a hug? More. A visit from Clara, the female baboon down the University lab hallway? More.

The work was steady, the pay excellent. Sunny stroked my hair and listened as I taught deeper communication. More + a noun. Show what you want. I recoiled visibly when he signed "more" and cupped his genitals lasciviously. My gesture was reflexive, not meant to scold, but Sunny signed "Sorry, Dave."

We—I—published papers on the bond between human trainer and baboon trainee. My last article, *Who's the Monkey Now? Primate-Based ASL*

THE STORY I TELL MYSELF ABOUT MYSELF

Breakthroughs, won two cash awards. Sunny was heralded as a genius for combining signs into long sentences. His slow, sweeping arms bore unexpected stories. *You look somewhat peaked today, are you feeling all right? I miss my mother and cousins but never knew my father; better that way, mother said. This classy-assed bowler hat showcases my impressive brain.*

Sunny and I traveled to Russia on a grant to share my—our—research. My girlfriend, Suzette, joined us. Sunny tolerated her, but clearly wanted my undivided attention over borscht and pierogi served on wobbly restaurant tables. He did not care for vodka, or our appreciation of it. The return flight from St. Petersburg was a comedy of misunderstanding about seating arrangements. Suzette stroked my forearm, picked lint off my shoulder, assured me that Sunny would get over sitting in cargo. When she turned to the gate agent, Sunny signed, *Tell me what you love about Suzette.*

After Russia, things changed. His signs retreated to monosyllables.

Sad. Heart. Hurt.

The medical team ran tests. Significant ventricle deterioration. Sunny was one of the university's biggest assets. So was I, assured the provost: Sunny's heart would be transferred to me free of charge.

Suzette wants to shave my chest. We prepare Sunny with scrubs, shower cap, mask. He lies in bed and asks for the TV remote instead of his books. We watch reruns of *Quincy* and I cringe during autopsy scenes. Sunny signs to me alone.

Love. Heart. Dave.

I nod, chin to chest, thinking about what beats inside me, what moves my blood. Thinking but not signing: Goodbye.

Author Note

Sarah Layden is the author of the novel *Trip Through Your Wires*. Her short fiction has appeared in *Boston Review, Artful Dodge, Stone Canoe, Blackbird,* and elsewhere, with nonfiction in *Salon, Ladies' Home Journal, The Humanist,* and other publications. She is an Assistant Professor of creative writing at Indiana University-Perdue University Indianapolis, and also teaches at the Indiana Writers Center.

www.ingramcontent.com/pod-product-compliance
Lightning Source LLC
Chambersburg PA
CBHW021027120726
47905CB00009B/3215